RIDING HIGH

6/09

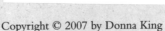

RIDING HIGH

DONNA KING

KINGFISHER
NEW YORK

Chapter 1

"Hey, Valentine, back off!" Billie Mason grinned at her horse. He was nudging her into a corner of the stall, nosing in her jacket pocket for a carrot. At 16.1 hands, he towered over her.

"I said beat it!" she insisted, ducking out of his way. "I have work to do here!"

The gray gelding turned and nudged her again as she continued mucking out.

Joey Hicks glanced in over the stall door. "You can leave that, Billie," he called. "That's my job!"

Billie put down the broom and brushed wisps of wavy dark hair away from her warm cheeks. "I'm finished anyway," she called back. "No thanks to Val. He keeps on pestering me for treats!"

"Aye, well, Valentine's Kiss is fat enough already, so don't give him any extra," little Joey warned. He was an ex-National Hunt jockey—a wizened stick of a man with sunken cheeks and cropped gray hair, now working as a stable boy in Matthew Pinkerton's training and competition stable.

"Sshh!" Billie warned, reaching up and pretending to cover Val's ears. "Watch who you're calling fat!" She left the stall and followed Joey outside the stable.

"Val's vain about his looks," she explained. "He takes these insults to heart."

Joey shrugged. "It's not my fault he's not competing this year," he reminded her. "All he does is laze around, eating and putting on weight."

"He's not fat!" Billie insisted. "Anyway, I still ride him loads!"

Joey picked up a hose and ran water into a plastic bucket. "Yes, you take him on trails when you feel like it," he acknowledged.

"But it's not the same as jumping him and getting him to work out in the dressage ring."

Billie frowned and watched the clear jet of water swirl into the bucket. "You don't really think he's overweight?" she checked. Across the barn, Val kicked impatiently at his stall door.

"If you don't work him hard enough, he's bound to lose condition." Joey always told it like it was. "Anyway, young Billie, why aren't you eventing this season? Valentine is far and away the best horse in the stable. It's a pity to let that talent go to waste."

It was Billie's turn to shrug. "Maybe next year," she mumbled.

"Hi, Billie." The stable manager, Matthew Pinkerton, came out of his office to talk to Joey. "Quite the stranger around here, aren't you?"

Billie raised her eyebrows. "How come everyone is getting on me all of a sudden?"

Luckily, her cell phone rang, and she walked a safe distance away to answer it. "Hey, Kirsty . . . Yeah, I'm at the stable . . . No, nothing much . . . Yeah, okay, outside Gap . . . See you there." She slipped the phone back inside her pocket and zipped up her coat.

Val kicked the door again. *What about me?* he seemed to say. *Are we going on a trail ride or what?*

Billie fussed and patted him as she passed by his door. "Not today," she told him. "Kirsty just called. I arranged to meet her in town."

Val tossed his head and snorted. His silky white mane swished across his dappled gray neck. He stamped his feet.

"Maybe tomorrow," Billie said vaguely, giving him one last pat. She nodded a farewell to the two riders who were walking their horses into the stable after a morning ride. "See you, Jules. See you, Bryony."

The two girls watched her leave.

"What's happened to Billie?" Jules demanded, dismounting from her new chestnut thoroughbred, Mission Impossible, otherwise known as Missie.

Bryony didn't like to gossip about her best friend. "What do you mean?"

"Why doesn't she ride with us like she used to? More to the point—how come she's not eventing anymore?"

"Leave Billie alone," Bryony muttered as she slid to the ground. She patted her black gelding, Christopher Columbus— Christy—and then slipped the bit from his mouth. "She's getting it from all directions— Matthew, Joey, her parents. And now you!"

"What did I say?" Jules protested as she unsaddled Missie. "Anyway, I didn't know the others were giving her a hard time."

"Well, they are," Bryony said. She watched Billie get onto her bike and ride off. "She just needs some space to clear her head, that's all."

* * *

Downtown was packed. Shoppers herded into the Gap. Billie checked her watch for the fifth time.

"Sorry I'm late!" Kirsty pushed toward her through the crowds. "I bumped into Karl Evans and his friends. Do you fancy meeting up with them at Starbucks?"

"Okay," Billie muttered. *Actually, no!* she thought. *Since Bryony's party, Karl Evans is the last person I want to hang out with!* But she didn't say anything.

"Cool. Because I said we'd see them there in half an hour." Taking Billie's arm, Kirsty bustled her through the glass doors of the store toward the jeans section. "Mum gave me money to buy some new skinnies!" she gushed.

"Cool," Billie said with a nod, wishing that she'd gotten changed out of her riding clothes. But Kirsty had set the time to meet and Billie had had to dash straight there. Then Kirsty had been 20 minutes late, so

Billie would have had time to pop home and change after all. *Do I smell like a horse?* she wondered.

Kirsty ran through the racks and then tried on six pairs of jeans. "No. No. Deffo not!" She came out of the dressing room empty-handed. "Let's go," she cried.

Billie trailed after her out of the Gap, following her down the street to Starbucks.

I definitely smell like a horse! she decided. There were traces of manure on her boots and smudges of horse snot on her coat. "Listen, you go ahead," she said to Kirsty at the door of Starbucks. Karl and his friends were already inside. "I need to buy a—a magazine!"

"Hey, don't leave me!" Kirsty panicked— she wasn't so in-your-face confident after all. It seemed that she needed Billie for backup.

"Okay, I'll buy the magazine later." A black cloud settled over Billie as she followed Kirsty. Karl Evans would blank her. His friends would be wearing stupid grins. Yep, sure enough . . .

"Hey, Kirsty!" Karl made room for her on the seat next to him. Billie was left standing beside Henry Webb.

And soon Kirsty didn't need backup at all. She was chatting to Karl, cozying up to him, not giving Billie another thought.

Henry was sniffing hard and grinning up at Billie. "Is that the sweet whiff of horse manure?" he asked in a loud, fake-innocent voice.

Billie was out of there in a flash, unlocking her bike from the stand outside and heading back to the stable. She preferred the company of Valentine's Kiss any day of the week to that of annoying boys making stupid remarks.

Soon she was out of town and riding back to her beloved Val, planning the route of their afternoon ride in her head.

"Billie Mason used to be a great rider,"

Jules said to Joey as she brushed Missie. In Joey Hicks, she'd found someone who loved a good gossip session.

The groom threw a light blanket over Missie's broad back and then buckled the girth straps. "Tell me about it," he grumbled. "That girl knows how to handle herself on horseback, no doubt about it."

"So what's the big mystery?" Jules wanted to know. "Why has she given up on eventing?"

Joey sniffed. "Boys?" he suggested darkly. "Maybe she found out that there's more to life than tail bandages and worming."

"Boys?" Jules echoed. She pictured Billie's wild, wavy blond hair, her shy smile and bright hazel eyes, her lousy fashion sense. "No way!"

"It happens," Joey muttered.

"Not to Billie Mason." Jules was completely sure. There was the famous Karl Evans fumble at Bryony's party—everyone knew that he'd tried to kiss her, because they'd seen Billie smack him across the face, and afterward Karl had dissed Billie and it had been all over the school. "Maybe she lost her nerve."

"That happens, too," Joey agreed. He put a halter on Missie, ready to lead her out to the farrier who had just arrived. "I've seen top professional jockeys take a fall and never get back in the saddle again. Something snaps inside their heads. They never get over it."

Billie rode up the lane between tall hawthorns heavy with white blossoms. Horses gazed idly over the gates. The archway above the entrance to the stalls was draped with pink clematis.

"Hi, I'm back!" she whispered to Val as she propped her bike up against a wall.

"Joey says Billie Mason lost her nerve," Jules reported to Bryony outside Christy's stall. "It's a mental thing."

Bryony put up a warning hand and turned away toward the tack room.

Jules followed her. "I thought Billie was your best friend. Don't you want to hear Joey's theory about why she stopped competing?"

"No."

"Why not? He knows what he's talking about. He says Valentine's Kiss is the best six-year-old warmblood he's ever seen. He has a fantastic jumping technique for cross-country and great paces for dressage—better than most thoroughbreds, according to Joey."

"I know all that," Bryony said abruptly. She hung Christy's bridle from its hook. "So what?"

"So it can't be Val that's the problem," Jules pointed out. "It's got to be Billie and whatever's going on inside her head."

Bryony faced Jules. "You're enjoying this, aren't you? One of your main rivals at the junior trials suddenly drops out of the circuit and you're grinning like the cat that got the cream."

"No, really, I'm not!"

"Yes, you are, Jules. If Billie is having a hard time for some reason, why not try a little sympathy instead of poking your nose in where it's not wanted?"

"Hey, take it easy!" Jules put up her hands in mock surrender. She followed close behind Bryony as the other girl strode out of the tack room.

Billie was just sliding back the bolt on Val's door. She heard raised voices and turned to see Jules tailing Bryony.

"What's gotten into you, Bryony?" Jules demanded in a voice that carried all the way across the barn.

Matthew Pinkerton was deep in conversation with the farrier. Joey Hicks was holding Missie, ready for shoeing.

Jules didn't see Billie, but even if she had, she insisted later, she would still have said what she did because it was true. "All I'm saying is that Billie Mason has lost her nerve. She doesn't have the guts for three-day eventing anymore. You know it, I know it, and everyone who knows anything about the sport knows it, too!"

Chapter 2

"Did you ride today?" Billie's mother asked when she got home early that evening.

"Mmm."

"Where did you go?"

"Along the bridle path," Billie muttered.

"Was it nice?"

Billie kicked off her boots and threw them out onto the porch where their Jack Russell terrier, Nipper, growled, pounced, and wrestled with them. "Nice!" she echoed sarcastically. "Yeah, Mum, it was 'nice.'"

"Don't be rude to your mother," Billie's dad grunted over the top of his newspaper. "You're lucky we still take an interest in your riding after what's happened this year."

"Nothing's happened," Billie retorted. *Leave me alone, why don't you?*

"Exactly," her dad pointed out. "Nothing. One big, fat zero."

"Don't start," Billie's mother pleaded. "If Billie has decided not to compete, we can't force her."

"Exactly." Billie copied her dad's sarcastic tone. Already the good mood she'd built up from riding Val along the riverbank had fizzled out. She was back in the deep hole that Jules Carter's accusation had thrown her into earlier that afternoon. *Billie Mason has lost her nerve!*

"What a waste." Billie's dad shook his head and retreated behind his paper.

It's impossible to talk to him, Billie thought despairingly. *Even if I could put it into words, how would he ever understand?*

"Were you by yourself or did Bryony ride with you?" Her mother tried to pretend that everyone's mood was bright and sunny, like the weather. "Will baked potatoes and salad be okay for supper? How much homework do you still have to do before school on Monday?"

Everyone knows Billie Mason has lost her nerve!

Billie was in her bedroom, cuddled up on the bed with Nipper, still reliving that toe-curling moment when Jules had dissed her in public.

Bryony had spotted Billie first and tried to stop Jules. Matthew Pinkerton had looked up and waited for Billie to rise to the challenge. He'd been disappointed when Billie had simply shrugged and disappeared inside Val's stall.

"Forget it," Bryony had said after Jules's dad had picked her up. "Jules always was jealous of you."

Billie had continued brushing Val and picking out his hooves. "I don't care," she'd said through gritted teeth. "Jules Carter can say what she likes. People can believe anything they want."

Ouch! she thought now, lying on her bed, stroking the terrier, and staring at the ceiling. The comment had hurt like crazy. *Who am I trying to kid?*

On the wall at the head of her bed there was a poster-size print of Valentine's Kiss flying over the water jump in the final event of last year's season. The photographer had captured him head-on, plunging into the water, en route to his individual junior gold medal.

Val's nostrils were flared wide and he was kicking up spray. Billie was leaning well back in the saddle with a look of total concentration on her face. Looking ahead for the next jump, she recalled now. Ready to gallop flat out up the hill and over the last fence to snatch the winner's medal.

On another wall, next to the closet, were pictures of her and Val at Bramham, Chatsworth, and Richmond. Of Billie in her black show-jumping jacket, of Val wearing his new saddle, his tack gleaming, his mane braided to perfection.

Inside the closet hung that slim, tailored jacket, next to Billie's white shirt and jodhpurs. Her long black leather boots, as shiny as ever, were wrapped in tissue paper and stored away with her show caps and gloves.

I folded up my life and packed it away, she thought. I mothballed my future and I can't explain why.

Bryony called Billie early the next morning. "Come out for a ride."

"Sorry, I can't," Billie said. She was still in her pajamas, staring at the pile of homework that she hadn't done.

"It's sunny. We could join the cross-country ride setting off from Fentsham at ten o'clock. Come on, Billie, get your act together!"

In spite of her jitters and doubts, Billie was tempted. "Whose trailer would we use?" she asked.

"Mine," Bryony said quickly. "Mum says she'll drive us. Get over to the stable as fast as you can."

Sunshine. Green fields. Riding Val through the bluebell woods behind Fentsham village. Billie pictured the perfect ride. "Okay," she agreed. "I'll be there in half an hour."

"We're off!" Bryony's mother announced, inching forward out of the stable yard onto the lane.

Beside her in the Land Rover, Billie and Bryony checked that they had their cell phones, helmets, and body protectors. In the trailer, Val and Christy were safely tethered for the short drive.

Before the horses had time to get bored or agitated, they were driving into the field at the start of the Fentsham ride.

"Glad you came?" Bryony asked as they unloaded Val and Christy.

The field was thronged with horses and

riders—cobs and Connemaras, piebalds and Palaminos. Riders wore numbered bibs to identify themselves to the officials.

Billie nodded happily. "Val's excited, too," she said with a grin. "This is his idea of a perfect day out—open countryside, no fences to jump, no pressure."

Val pranced across the lush grass, head up, ears pricked, eager to start the ride. The moment that Billie was in the saddle, he hustled through the crowd of riders toward the starting point.

"That's a lovely horse you have there," an official with a clipboard told Billie, taking in Val's graceful conformation, proud, arched neck, and dappled coloring. "Is he a thoroughbred?"

She smiled. "No, he's a Dutch warmblood."

"Looks to me like he'd make a good eventer," the official said.

Billie blushed and then rode on.

"Oops!" Bryony said, catching up with her on Christy. "There's no getting away from it, is there?"

"Val's way too handsome for his own good," Billie joked. She posted to a trot as Val surged forward until there were no horses ahead of him. "And he likes to be at the front!"

"Too true," Bryony agreed. Secretly, she had to admit that her own Christopher Columbus, as much as she loved him, wasn't in the same league as Valentine's Kiss.

Quickly they settled into the ride, cantering across open fields, crossing lanes, trotting through bluebell woods.

"So cool!" Billie breathed in the scent of the flowers. There was a carpet of blue beneath the trees, small brooks to jump, low branches to duck underneath, and 15 uninterrupted miles ahead of them.

"Better than homework?" Bryony teased.

"Better than anything I can think of!" Billie replied.

Just then two riders hustled them from behind, tailgating them and then letting their horses barge past Val and Christy.

"Sorry," one of the women muttered as she fought to control her big Welsh cob. She pulled hard on the reins, but her horse rode through the bit, veering off the path deep into the bluebells and then up a steep hill. The girls could tell that the rider wasn't in control of her horse.

"Looks like she's got a problem," Bryony muttered to Billie.

The cob reared and then took off up the hill, trampling the flowers and breaking into a gallop.

"That's not Pam's horse," her friend explained. She was struggling to control her horse, too. "It's her first ride for ages."

"It will be her last, if she doesn't watch out," Billie muttered. She watched the cob gallop to the top of the hill and then disappear over the ridge. By now, his rider had lost hold of the reins completely and was slumped forward, clinging onto the horse's mane. "Wait here," she told Bryony and the other woman, clicking her tongue to urge Val on up the hill. He responded with a smooth trot. Then, when she asked him to canter, he sat back on his haunches and launched forward, gathering speed as they reached the brow of the hill.

From there, Billie could once more see the runaway cob. "Probably heading for home," Billie said to herself as she watched him plunge down the hill and across a stream. His rider still clung to his neck, reins flapping, both feet out of the stirrups. Ahead of them there was a clearing littered with huge piles of logs.

Disaster! Billie thought. Her heart rate increased as she saw the danger. *He's going to take a flying jump and that woman's going to break her neck, unless I can cut them off!*

Digging her heels into Val's sides, she galloped after the runaway horse. She chose a downhill course that took her under low branches, weaving between trees to gain ground. It was more direct than the route taken by the other horse, and they started to gain on them. Val's hooves thudded into the soft earth. He stretched out his neck, flared his nostrils, and galloped like the wind.

"Whoa!" Pam's high, scared voice drifted back toward Billie.

Her horse ignored her, eyes rolling, ears laid flat on his head. He wanted to get rid of the clumsy burden that clung to his neck.

Skillfully, Billie steered Val between the oak trees. Horse and rider soared over the stream, making up ground with every step.

The cob had almost reached the clearing. His eyes were on the first giant log pile. He gathered himself, ready to sail clean over it.

But Billie and Val charged ahead and cut him off just in time, forcing him off course, pushing him back the way that he'd come, and bringing him to a halt in a thicket of impenetrable willows.

The runaway horse's sides were heaving and sweating. Pam slithered from his back, bending over, gasping for breath.

"Are you okay?" Quickly, Billie dismounted and ran across to catch hold of the cob's reins. Behind her, she heard Bryony calling her name and the sound of more hooves approaching.

Pam groaned and then nodded. "If he'd taken off over those logs, I'd have been a goner!"

"You're sure you're not hurt?"

"I'm fine. Just shaken up. Thank you." The woman straightened up and then took a deep breath. "Really, thank you!"

"Nice job, Billie!" Bryony called as she joined them. "That was one great piece of riding!"

"Just like the old days," Billie said, grinning.

And it was true—back there in those woods she'd felt the familiar thrill of cross-country riding, with the wind on her face, the blur of the dark tree trunks, golden flashes of sunlight breaking through the canopy of leaves overhead.

Bryony grinned back. "Wait till I tell Jules Carter what you just did!"

"Whatever," Billie replied with a shrug. She went back to Val, gathered his reins, and then stepped back up into the saddle. "Good boy!" she told him.

Bryony rode up beside her and leaned sideways. "I'll tell her one thing for sure," she confided. "There's nothing wrong with your nerve, Billie!"

Billie dropped the smile and grew deadly serious. "No," she said, patting Val's smooth neck, "I never said there was!"

Chapter 3

"I don't get it!" Billie's dad had arrived at the stable to pay for Valentine Kiss's expenses. He'd overheard Bryony excitedly telling Matthew Pinkerton the story of Billie and Val's heroic rescue. Now he took Billie to one side. "How come you waste your time trail riding instead of getting back into some serious training?" he hissed.

"I'm not wasting my time," Billie argued. "The Fentham ride was good exercise for Val. He needs plenty of work."

Her dad refused to listen. "And it's not just *your* time you're wasting on these pleasure rides. Remember—it's Val's fitness that you're putting at risk with these flashy heroics!"

Billie gasped. "I can't believe you just said that!"

"It's true. Galloping a valuable horse through those woods off the track was a stupid thing to do." The money that James had just handed over to the trainer had made a big dent in his bank account. His focus was on how much the horse was worth and the cost of keeping him at a top stable.

"Oh, right—next time I'll let the woman fall off and break her neck," Billie muttered. She felt tears sting her eyes as she tried to walk away.

"Listen to me, Billie." Her father followed her outside the stable. "That reckless streak of yours has always been a problem, ever since you rode your first pony. I always said it would get you into trouble."

"Well, it hasn't," she retorted, turning to face him. "Name one accident I've had because of my so-called recklessness. Name one injury Val has had!"

"Reckless—and stubborn," her dad went on, ignoring her. "Every time I try to give you some sound advice, it turns into a battle of wills."

Billie took a deep breath and then let her shoulders slump. "Okay, Dad, if that's the way you want to look at it."

"It's the only way," he insisted, his sharp features set hard. "Ask Matthew. I'm sure he agrees with me."

"What's that?" Hearing his name mentioned, the trainer came across with the young, fair-haired woman he'd been talking to. "James, this is Sarah Norwood. She's a friend of mine who's spending some time at the stable. She's a top horse trainer in New Zealand, and I've brought her in to coach the girls. Sarah, meet Billie Mason and her dad."

James and Sarah shook hands. "I was just telling Billie a few home truths," James explained.

Billie grimaced at her dad's tactics. *That's*

right—show me up in front of a stranger, why don't you?

"She needs to listen to some good professional advice," James went on. "To tell you the truth, Matthew, I've given up trying to get through to Billie. It's you she needs to hear it from."

The trainer shot Billie a sideways glance. "What do you need to hear from me?" he asked in his clipped, factual way. As usual, he looked immaculate in his pale blue polo shirt with the dark red and gold Pinkerton logo, jeans, and jodhpur boots.

"How I don't care about my horse and how reckless I am!" Billie burst out, her lips trembling. The steady gaze of Sarah Norwood only made her feel more horrible. "Plus the fact that I'm a fool for giving up eventing and how it costs a fortune to keep Val here. You name it, I'm doing it wrong!"

"Ah!" Matthew said, glancing quickly from daughter to father and back again. "It sounds to me like you two have a lot to sort out. Sarah and I will leave you to it."

"Sorry, I didn't mean to drag you in," Billie said with a sigh.

The trainer nodded. "That's okay." He turned away and then seemed to change his mind. "I will say one thing, though, James. In my opinion, Billie isn't a reckless rider. In fact, quite the opposite—she always keeps a cool head and she rides with faultless judgment."

Billie took a deep breath to stop herself from hugging prim, stiff-upper-lip Matthew. "Thank you!" she breathed.

Sarah Norwood watched her face carefully.

James Mason took in the top trainer's praise and promptly turned it against his daughter. "Then I'm back to my original point—what a waste! A waste of talent, Billie. And a waste of money if you're not competing!"

Rewind. Play it back. Always the same

old tune. Billie looked her father in the eyes. "Read my lips, Dad. I'm not competing with Val. You can't make me. I don't want to do it. Not now, not next week. Not ever again!"

"What happened to you at Starbucks on Saturday?" Kirsty asked Billie at school the following morning. She was strutting down a corridor at the head of a group that included Karl and Henry. "I looked around and you were gone!"

"Yeah, I had stuff to do," Billie muttered. All eyes were on her. None were friendly.

"She had to buy more *parfum de cheval*!" Karl snickered, digging Henry in the ribs.

"Funny!" Billie glared at him.

"Neigh!" Henry whinnied as the gang walked on, leaving Billie choking back tears.

Hey, Billie, Bryony texted during morning break. *Will be at the stable at 6. C u there? X*

Maybe, Billie texted back.

No maybes—be there! Bryony replied.

What's the point? Billie thought. Her mind had wandered off during English class, and she was deep in the problems that she was having at home.

"Billie, your mother and I have been talking," her dad had told her the previous evening after the face-off at the stable. "I want you to sit down and listen carefully to what we've decided."

"Billie, what do you think the poet means when he writes about the pen 'snug as a gun' in his hand?" Mr. Bolton, the English teacher, asked. ". . . Billie?"

Billie was lost in remembering how she'd sat down on the couch with a huge feeling of foreboding.

"I don't have to tell you how expensive it is to keep Valentine's Kiss at Matthew's stable," her dad had said. "Of course, we were prepared to make the financial sacrifice because Matthew is the best and because you showed such promise as a young rider. Everyone said that you and Val had the potential to reach the very top."

". . . Billie?" Mr. Bolton came up to her. He noticed that her hands were shaking. "You look pale. Are you okay?"

She nodded.

"Are you sure?" the teacher asked.

Billie's mother had sat down next to her on the couch, trying to take hold of her hand. Billie had pulled away.

"But now that you've taken the unilateral decision not to compete," her dad went on, "your mother and I are in agreement that we should stop paying these astronomical fees and take Val out of the stable as soon as possible. In other words, at the end of this month."

Billie had sat in silence as her whole world crashed down. Her dad had sounded so reasonable. Her mother had looked so sorry, but she never argued with Billie's dad. When he said that they were in agreement, he really meant that he'd made up his mind.

"Of course, we'll find a decent alternative for Valentine," her dad had gone on. "We won't just abandon him. He'll go to a good home."

Alternative . . . abandon . . . home? "Do you mean you're going to sell him?" she'd whispered.

"We have to," her dad had said. "I'm sorry, Billie, but if you're not going to compete, we simply can't justify the expense."

Sitting at her desk, Billie's head swam. Everything went blurry.

Mr. Bolton looked around the classroom. "Kirsty, Billie isn't well. Would you take her to the nurse's office, please? Quickly . . . Can you stand up, Billie? Careful! . . . Lucy, we need an extra hand here. Watch out, Karl—move your chair . . ."

Billie went to the stable after school

because she didn't want to go home.

The school secretary had been about to call her mother to say that she'd fainted, but Billie had insisted that she was okay— she didn't need to go home. All she needed was a drink of water. "See, I'm fine!" she'd said, getting up from the bed in the nurse's office.

She'd gotten through the day by blocking Val from her mind, concentrating her hardest on writing an essay on the imagery used by Seamus Heaney in the poem "Digging," watching a video about World War I, and observing her chemistry teacher doing things with test tubes and Bunsen burners.

But now, as she leaned her bike against a wall and walked over to Val's stall, she had to face the facts.

"Hey!" she whispered sadly as Val poked his head over the door. "Yes, it's me."

He tossed his head and stamped impatiently.

"Steady," she murmured. She stroked his soft muzzle and then made a fist and rubbed his forehead with her knuckles. "You like that, don't you?"

The horse closed his eyes and sighed.

"It's Billie, isn't it?" a voice asked, and she turned to see Sarah, the new trainer. She was leading Missie out of the indoor ring, wearing her white polo shirt tucked neatly into the slim waistband of her jeans. She looked tanned and in shape from working in the open air.

"Yes, hi," she answered, blushing at the memory of the argument that the trainer had witnessed. Obviously, Sarah realized that she'd stopped competing, though she didn't know yet that Billie would have to sell Valentine's Kiss. No one did.

"How's it going?"

"Good, thanks." *Block everything out—don't let anyone in*. Billie slid the bolt and stepped inside Val's stall.

"Great horse." Sarah stopped to admire

the gray. "I lunged him in the ring before I started working with Missie. He's pretty athletic."

"Thanks." Billie waited with dread for the next question—why don't you compete anymore, blah-blah-blah?

Instead, Sarah walked Missie to her stall. A couple of minutes later, when Billie had saddled Val and tacked him up, ready for a quiet trail ride, she reappeared. "Hey, Billie, one thing I did admire when I was lunging Valentine was how straight and well balanced he is. Plus, he's so easy to handle."

Billie nodded. "He loves to learn," she explained. "Whenever you teach him something new, he's right there with you. The only time he tightens up and gets tense is if I let him come too fast to a fence in the show-jumping ring. But I guess that's my fault, not his."

Sarah nodded. "Did you ever use canter poles in front of a practice fence? That'd slow him down and improve his fluency at the same time."

"Good idea," Billie agreed.

"Do you want to try it?" Sarah asked, opening the stall door for her.

"Now?"

"Yeah, why not?"

Billie could have given her a dozen answers—because I'm not in the mood, I haven't taken Val into the ring for more than a month, I'm not competing anymore, and besides, in four short weeks I have to sell him to a stranger who might not take good care of him or let him get bitten and kicked by other horses! But for some unknown reason, she said, "Yeah, why not?" and followed Sarah outside the stable.

"Which fence does Val have the most difficulty with?" she asked, standing back and letting Billie trot Val between the fences.

"It's usually the rail–ditch–rail combination," she explained. "He doesn't mind ditches in themselves, but he likes to be able to see them before he jumps. If there's a rail in the way, it bothers him."

"So he rushes at the combination to get it over with, to get himself back inside his comfort zone. But by then he's lost his equilibrium and you have to take the time to bring him up again for the next fence."

As she talked, Sarah laid four striped poles on the ground leading to the ditch, spacing them far enough apart for Valentine's Kiss to put in one full stride between each. "Keep him on a tight rein as you approach the first pole," she instructed. "As soon as he slows down, release the pressure and let him find his own way over the second, third, and fourth. Then he'll be up and over the combination, no problem."

"Okay, we're ready," Billie called as she lined up Val. She set him off at a trot, increasing to a canter, keeping good contact with his mouth until he slowed at the pole as Sarah had predicted. Then she lengthened the reins.

Smoothly, Val cantered over the poles, concentrating on his feet so that he didn't have time to worry about the hidden ditch ahead. When he reached the rail, he launched himself easily over the combination and landed perfectly on the far side.

"Beautiful!" Sarah called. "Now do it again!"

The new trainer worked with Billie and Val for half an hour before she was satisfied.

"Okay, you won't have any more problems with these combinations," she assured Billie as she led Val back to his stable. "Remember, when you ask a horse to carry out any task, it's about making sure that the easiest way to go is the right way. And about taking off the pressure the split second that he gets it. Oh, and about keeping your shape, staying in balance, having soft hands, and having an intuitive understanding of the way the horse's mind works."

"Not much to work on there, then," Billie said with a laugh, feeling the tension of the last several days melt away.

Sarah held open the stall door and looked at her intently.

"What?" Billie asked, suddenly feeling self-conscious.

"Nothing," Sarah said with a quick grin. "But I knew you could smile if you tried!"

"Hi, Billie!" A call from Bryony saved Billie from having to answer. It was true, working with Val had made her feel happy again, but she didn't want to explain her problems to the new trainer.

"Is that your friend?" Sarah asked.

Billie nodded. "Her mum just dropped her off."

Sarah gave Val a good, firm pat on the neck. "Good work, guys," she said before disappearing inside the office.

Bryony rushed up to Billie. "Hey, did you just get to work with Sarah Norwood?"

"Yeah, she's cool," Billie muttered, distracted. She needed to brush down Val and see that he had fresh hay.

"Cool doesn't quite cut it!" Bryony exclaimed, her gray eyes shining. "Try 'numero uno'!"

Billie looked up from fastening the girth on Val's turnout blanket. "Huh?"

"Sarah Norwood is way more than cool!" Bryony insisted. "She's only come over all the way from New Zealand, where she's been the number-one horse trainer for the last five years, working with all the very best stables. She only worked on horse-whispering techniques with Monty Roberts in California!"

Billie stood up and rested a hand against Val's withers. "Wow!" she said quietly.

"Yes, wow!" Bryony insisted. "And she

worked with you, you lucky thing! You just had a session with one of the top teachers of natural horsemanship in the whole world!"

Chapter 4

Billie read the grade for her Seamus Heaney essay—a C minus.

"I got a B plus!" Kirsty hissed.

"Disappointing effort," Mr. Bolton said as he handed back Billie's work. "I see you as an A student, Billie, but this was well below par. Let's put it down to the fact that you weren't feeling well during class on Monday."

Billie nodded and kept her head down for the rest of the day.

And if things weren't going well at school, they were ten times worse at home. Her mother was stressed out and nagging Billie bigtime, while her dad's black mood had crept into every corner of the house.

"Talk to him," her mother pleaded with Billie. "Explain. Don't cut yourself off."

"There's nothing to explain," was Billie's stubborn reply.

"He wants to know why you're willing to sacrifice Val because of your stubbornness."

But Billie would shake her head and rush off to the stable or to catch the bus to school instead of letting her dad give her a ride as usual. She knew her mother was caught in the middle, but too bad! If she couldn't help save Val, Billie wasn't interested in making her life easier.

In fact, the only time the cloud lifted was when she was with Val. "I'll spend every spare second with you," she murmured in his ear on Friday after school. She was counting the days until the end of the month, willing time to stand still.

"Here again?" Sarah Norwood greeted Billie as she and Jules walked Mission

Impossible toward the indoor ring. "We can't keep you away!"

"Hey, Billie, come and watch Sarah work with Missie," Jules suggested. "I already invited Bryony. You two can pick up a few tips if you like."

So Billie joined Bryony and Jules to watch the trainer lunge the young chestnut mare, noting how Sarah took her back to basics, asking her to move out on a circle around her in the big ring.

"Simple exercises can show big problems," Sarah explained. "Look how she's raising her head and fighting me. It means she's not ready to submit. So I just stay calm and wait for her head to go down."

"Nice work," Bryony said when Missie eventually lowered her head.

"Now she has a softer-looking eye," Sarah pointed out as Missie trotted at the end of her lunge line, close to the girls. "She's saying to me, 'Okay, you're the boss.'"

After ten minutes of hard, simple work, Sarah drew in the line and walked Missie across to Jules. "She's a new horse, right?"

Jules nodded. "I got her just before Christmas. She's a half sister to Free Spirit, the horse I lost at the end of last season."

"I didn't know that!" Billie whispered to Bryony.

"From the same mare," Bryony told her.

"I haven't really bonded with her yet," Jules went on.

Sarah patted Missie. "Mares are often more aggressive than geldings, but she has to learn that you call the shots."

Jules nodded. "I know. But I have to work her in for ages before an event; otherwise she won't settle. Then when we get in the ring, in front of the crowd and the judges, she starts throwing herself around again."

"Sounds like she's an adrenaline junkie!" Sarah grinned. "It's the tension of the big event that's winding her up. We'll work on that the next time." Handing the lunge line over to Jules, she let her walk Missie back to her stable. "Who's next?" she asked Bryony and Billie.

"You go," Bryony said. "I have to wait for the vet to give Christy his shots."

So Billie tacked up Val and rode him into the show-jumping ring.

"I want to see you jump the three-part complex at the far end," Sarah told her. "Take your time; relax. Do it in your normal way."

Calmly, Billie trotted Val between the high fences, watching his ears prick up and feeling him gather himself as she pointed him toward the triple. With a slight pressure against his flanks, she urged him forward.

He cantered at the first fence and flew over it, collected himself for the bend between the jumps, and soared again. Once more, and they were clear.

"Yep!" Sarah nodded and smiled. "I don't

think you need much help from me on that one!"

Billie trotted Val back. "Did he take the corner okay?"

"Perfect. You're a great team." Sarah reached up to examine Val's tack. "That's a nice bit you have on him."

"Yes, he has a soft mouth. I don't like to use harsh bits."

"Me neither. Gentle hands—that's what it's all about." There was a pause, and then Sarah went on. "You two have it all—you know that?"

"Except the confidence to enter him into competitions," Billie murmured. *Whoops—where did that come from?*

Sarah looked up at her. "How come?"

Why am I telling her this? she wondered as the words tumbled out. "I don't know. Last spring we were winning everything in sight. We moved up from prenovice to novice, and he didn't mind any technical difficulty that I threw at him. This spring we were aiming for the British junior team selection at Chepstow. It's three weeks from now."

"So what went wrong?" Sarah was genuinely curious.

"I can't explain. I wish I could." Billie took a deep breath. "It's like some big mental block."

"Here, dismount," Sarah suggested, holding Val's reins while Billie jumped to the ground.

She breathed in again. From nowhere her emotions were rising—the ones that she'd fought to keep down for a whole year.

"Tell me," Sarah said.

"It was the last three-day event of the season. We'd scored well in dressage and show jumping. In fact, we were in tied first place when we went into the cross-country."

"So did you win?"

Billie nodded. "But . . ."

Sarah waited in silence for Billie to go on.

"But after that I never wanted to compete again."

"Because?"

Billie shrugged. She felt ashamed of the tears that were brimming up and trickling down her cheeks. "You know they're saying that I lost my nerve?"

"Yeah, I heard. But I don't think it's that simple."

"I saw something horrible," she confessed. The words were as unstoppable as her tears. Why now? Why was she telling Sarah, after she'd succeeded in blocking it for all this time? "When I think of it, it still makes me feel sick!"

She waited again.

"The horse that rode cross-country ahead of us—it was Free Spirit."

"Jules's horse?"

Billie nodded. "They fell at a willow fence on the far side of the lake. I didn't see it happen, but I saw what went on afterward." She faltered and put her hand over her eyes.

"What did you see?" Sarah asked gently.

"I saw Jules. She was on her feet, and I could tell she was okay. But Free Spirit was still down, lying on her side. I knew she couldn't get up. The vet was already there." It was no use—Billie couldn't bear to describe the moment itself. Instead she sobbed.

"They had to destroy the horse." Sarah said it for her. "You saw them do it?"

"It was awful," Billie wept. "And Val and I went on over the willow fence and finished the course. We came first, but I knew it would be the last time because I'd seen what had happened to Free Spirit and I said no way would I ever do it again—never put Val at risk, never injure him or break his leg like Jules did with Free Spirit. I love my horse too much to lose him that way!"

"I understand," Sarah said. That was all.

Then she let Billie lead Val back to his stall.

She brushed Val and fussed over him, detangling his mane and working on it until it shone.

"Three more weeks," she murmured. Her arm ached from the brushing. Her heart was breaking.

Val gave a long, loud sigh of pleasure. He turned his head and nudged Billie's shoulder.

"I can't bear it!" she whispered. "I'm trapped in a maze. My mind turns this way and that, but there's no way out. I love you, Val, and I don't want to lose you. But I can't let what happened to Free Spirit happen to you. I'd never forgive myself!"

Val nudged her again.

"Hey, Billie," Sarah said, leaning over the stall door and ignoring her tear-stained face. "I just asked Jules and Bryony out for a dawn ride tomorrow morning. It'd be cool if you could come, too."

★ ★ ★

They set out in the gray light—four riders trotting briskly out of the stable, disappearing into the wet mist that clung to the riverbank.

"We're crazy!" Bryony shivered, zipping her jacket up under her chin. "We should still be in bed!"

"This fog is spooky!" Jules muttered.

Billie was up ahead with Sarah, who was riding Matthew's own gray gelding, Hawksmoor.

"You say Val doesn't mind water?" Sarah checked.

"He likes it," Billie assured her. She loved this before-dawn feeling. Birds were already singing in the bushes hidden by the mist. There was the faintest hint of pink in the eastern sky.

"Okay, Billie, lead us across the river," Sarah told her. "Come on, you guys!" she shouted to Bryony and Jules. "Follow Billie!"

She turned Val down the bank and waded him steadily across the swift current. Soon he was up to his belly, bold and sure-footed. He forged his way ahead, quickly reaching the far bank, and then waited for the rest.

"Good boy!" Billie leaned forward and patted him. The rising sun was beginning to cut through the mist. In the field ahead, a dozen gray rabbits took flight and headed for their burrows.

"Fancy a gallop?" Sarah asked after everyone had reached dry land. This time she chose Jules and Missie to lead the way.

Jules nodded and set off, galloping smoothly, soon followed by Bryony and Christy.

"Can you hold Val back?" Sarah checked.

Billie nodded.

Sarah and Hawksmoor set off, third in line.

Billie waited until the big gray reached a

gnarled hawthorn tree, and then she let Val go. She felt his hooves thunder over the ground as he seemed to break through the mist, up the hill into the clear air. He was powerful and steady as he gained on Sarah and the others, head stretched forward, racing straight and swift.

"Cool!" Jules was breathless as she pulled up at the top of the hill. The sun had risen above the far horizon. "Well done, Missie!"

"Look at that!" Bryony breathed, taking in the shimmering golden globe.

Sarah turned and waited for Billie. "How much fun is this?" she said with a grin.

"Lots!" Billie agreed. She pulled up in the middle of the bunch. It made her heart break, but she had to tell them the truth. "Confession time!" she announced, taking a deep breath. "I won't be able to ride out with you for much longer!"

"How come?" Bryony asked.

Billie leaned forward in the saddle to

pat Val's neck. "Dad says he won't keep paying for him," she explained. "In three weeks' time, Valentine's Kiss will be put up for sale."

Chapter 5

"Oh no, I can't believe it!" Bryony was stunned by the news.

"You poor thing!" Jules commiserated. "No wonder you've been grumpy lately."

Bryony frowned at her. "Thank you, Miss Tactful!" She brought Christy up alongside Billie. "Can't you persuade your dad to change his mind?"

Billie shook her head. "He says that if I don't compete with Val, he's not willing to shell out the money for his upkeep. We have to sell him—as simple as that."

Jules stared at her. "Then compete!"

"Yes," Bryony urged. "Get back into it, Billie. If it's the only way to keep Val, you can do it!"

"I can't. Sarah knows why." She turned to the trainer for support.

"Back off, girls," Sarah told them. "Billie has an issue with the competition part. She's dealing with it in her own way."

"Well, she'd better hurry up," Jules said, turning Missie for home. "Because if she doesn't deal with it before the end of the month, it'll be too late. Val will be history and there'll be no turning back!"

The ride home was subdued. The four riders walked their horses downhill in the early-morning sun.

"You're doing well," Sarah told Billie, hanging back behind Bryony and Jules. "You're beginning to face your demons."

"I am?" Billie asked. "It doesn't feel like it."

"Believe me, you are." Sarah nodded and rode ahead, leaving Billie to her thoughts.

When they reached the stable, they split off into their stalls and quietly untacked their horses.

"Good boy," Billie murmured to Val, unstrapping his girth.

Bryony stopped on her way to the tack room. "Billie, I don't know what to say. I'm just so sorry, believe me."

Jules followed soon after, walking on a couple of paces and then coming back. "I'm sorry, too," she said. "Really, I am. And I know I haven't been acting that nice toward you lately."

Billie looked up. "That's okay," she muttered. "I guess we've been too busy competing with each other. It was usually you against me in the final stages, wasn't it?"

Jules nodded. "Yeah—and more often than not, you won!"

"Well, not anymore," Billie said with a sad smile. "It's up to you and Missie to get onto the British junior team!"

Jules frowned. "Missie isn't ready. Like I said, we haven't bonded that well."

"Yeah, why is that?" Billie asked, coming up to the stall door. "She's a great horse."

"I know. But I guess it was a mistake buying the half sister of Free Spirit. I mean, Missie has the same paces. She feels the same when I ride her. So every time I get in the saddle, I think about poor Free Spirit."

This was the first time that Billie had heard Jules talk this way. "I know what you're saying. Do you miss her?" she asked.

"Totally," Jules admitted. "And I still blame myself for the fall. I rushed Free Spirit at that water jump. I pushed her at it to gain a few seconds, and when she landed, she was off balance. I heard her leg crack as she hit the ground. I knew right away what I'd done."

"Oh!" Billie was horrified.

"Honestly, I was in shock. Afterward, Matthew told me not to feel too bad—it can happen to the best riders. But I couldn't eat or sleep. I was a total mess."

"I'm sorry. I didn't realize."

"My mum and dad didn't know what to

do. It was Matthew who came to our house before Christmas and told us about Mission Impossible. He knew she was for sale. He said he thought the only way forward was to buy a new horse and get me back in the saddle again. We took his advice, and that's where I am now."

"Really, I didn't know what you'd gone through." Billie shook her head.

"It's not the sort of thing you talk about, is it?" Jules said.

"True." Billie allowed herself a wry smile. "But did you know that I was the rider who followed you that day? I actually saw what happened to Free Spirit."

"Wasn't it awful?" Jules's voice cracked as she put her hand up to her eyes.

"The worst," Billie whispered. "But you know what, Jules, you had the guts to pick yourself up and start again. And that's more than I can do!"

"If you put the pressure on in the wrong

way, the horse will resist," Sarah explained to Bryony, who was having a problem loading Christy into the trailer. "To get him in smoothly, first of all you have to look at it from the horse's point of view."

Billie leaned on the tack-room door, watching and listening.

"To Christy, that trailer looks like a dark, enclosed space with no exit. His natural instinct is to run away from it. The horse is a flight animal, remember."

Bryony took in the good advice.

"Never tug on his lead rope and try to force him in. Persuade him to trust you instead."

"See you, Billie!" Jules called as she ran out of the barn to her dad's Land Rover.

Billie nodded and waved. She remembered word for word what Jules had just told her. "Who'd have thought it?" she muttered. Her rival had always seemed so in-your-face competitive—kind of brittle. Now Billie knew better.

"Hold the lead rope slack in your hand," Sarah told Bryony. "Be patient. Let Christy stand and assess the situation for as long as he likes."

Bryony and Christy stood at the bottom of the ramp. The horse stared warily at the trailer and then gradually lowered his head to sniff the ground.

"Good work," Sarah said softly.

"But I didn't do anything," Bryony replied.

"You didn't have to," Sarah said with a smile. "Christy's ready. Lead him in."

"If you put pressure on in the wrong way, I'll resist." Billie had learned some important facts that morning. Back home, talking to her mother, she decided to share some of what she'd learned. "It's like Sarah says about horses—if you try to force me into doing something, my instinct is to run away!"

"But you're not a horse," her mother pointed out. "And your dad doesn't have money to burn while you mess around deciding whether or not you want to compete." She looked stressed, and Billie realized this situation was taking its toll on her parents, too.

"I know. This is just my way of trying to make you understand." Billie was sitting cross-legged on the bench in the laundry room. Her mother was busy folding clothes. Nipper wrestled with Billie's feet.

She changed direction. "Jules Carter was telling me that she was really broken up about Free Spirit's accident."

"Yes, I expect she was."

"Me, too." Billie paused for a moment and then went on. "I saw it all—the vet and everything."

"Did you, darling? I didn't realize." Her mother looked appalled.

"It was the worst thing—one second Free Spirit was alive and in so much pain. The next, she was dead—lifeless—just nothing. Unbelievable."

Mrs. Mason stopped folding and sat down next to Billie. "But at least the poor creature was out of her misery."

Billie nodded. She cleared her throat. "Mum, I've been thinking, and I've decided something. I want to talk to you and Dad together."

Her mother put her arm around her. "That sounds important. Let's go and find him."

"I've decided to start competing again," Billie said quietly.

For once her father wasn't watching TV or reading the financial columns in the newspaper.

"Ha!" James gave a triumphant cry. "I knew you'd come to your senses!"

"Don't you want to know why?" Billie asked him.

"It's obvious. I put on the pressure and threatened to sell your horse. You did a U-turn and decided to get back into the sport."

"Actually, no, that's not the reason. It was Jules Carter."

"Ha!" her dad said again. "That's my girl. The good old competitive spirit!"

"No, Dad. It was the opposite."

"Whatever. You've changed your mind. You're ready to start eventing again—that's all that matters."

Her dad was happy. He saw familiar signs of Billie's fighting spirit. She really was a chip off the old block.

"Your father was never very interested in psychology." For once Billie's mother teased her husband. "I have a lifetime's experience of observing him. But *I'm* interested, darling. You can explain it to me when you're ready to."

Chapter 6

"Let me check I'm getting this." Sarah stopped Billie in full flow. It was early on Sunday morning. No one else was in the yard. "You want to put Valentine's Kiss back in training for three-day eventing?"

Billie nodded eagerly. "Dad's changed his mind. As long as I do my best at what's left of this season's events, he's happy for me to keep him."

"Whoa, let me check on something." The trainer rolled back her sleeves and turned on the hose. "Grab that broom," she ordered. "What I want to know is whether you're deciding to compete again purely because of your fear of losing Val. Because if you are, that would be the wrong reason, and I wouldn't be happy to go ahead."

"No, honestly. Dad might think it is. But it wasn't like that. It had to do with our dawn ride, and before that, I had a chase through the woods on the trail ride. Val was so strong and sure-footed. I wasn't afraid for him anymore."

"Good," Sarah said. "Anything else?"

"I talked to Jules," she added.

"Good again. I don't need to know what you said. It's enough that you two talked." Sarah hosed down outside the stable and Billie swept. "Okay, Billie, we start with dressage, ten o'clock sharp."

"Let's look at that slow collected canter straight from walk," Sarah told Billie.

She and Val had gone through the full dressage test for Sarah, and now the trainer wanted to go back and concentrate on certain sections.

"Make sure there's no jerkiness. We need a smooth transition and then a half circle right for sixty feet."

Precisely and smoothly, Billie and Val performed the maneuver.

"Yes, good. Now Val's showing the desire to move forward. Your seat is perfect, Billie. Good work!"

She reined Val to a halt. "How about the flying change and collected canter left? We sometimes mess that up."

"No, it was fine. Try the five-step rein back again. That's it. Make sure Val accepts the contact. Good."

Billie smiled. Val was performing wonderfully. When she asked him to stop backing up and then go forward at medium walk, he was step perfect.

"You both look like you're having a good time out there," Sarah said. She was leaning on the fence, watching every move. "But we've been working for twenty minutes, and you can't ask your horse to concentrate for much longer than that. Let's call it a day."

"Thanks." Billie smiled as she rode out of the ring.

"Tell me something," Sarah said, looking thoughtful as she held open the gate. "Last year, did you and Val get onto the list of sixty-five?"

She knew that Sarah was talking about the list of juniors who would go forward that season for selection on the British team.

"Yes, we were on it," she confirmed. "But we've missed too many one-day events in March and April. There's only Ireton Castle coming up, so I guess we lost our chance for this year."

Sarah nodded. "Maybe. Maybe not. Let me talk to Matthew."

"Whoa!" Billie reined Val back and turned around. "Why? What are you thinking?"

Sarah shrugged. "I don't know for sure because I'm a rookie here in England. But maybe the selectors will make an exception."

"You think they'll let us compete at Chepstow?" Billie gasped. The three-day trial was the most important of the year. It was there that the selectors for the junior team made their final choices.

Sarah closed the gate and then walked across the yard with Billie and Val. "Let's hope so," she said quietly. "But if the answer is yes, Billie, it means you eat, sleep, and breathe eventing for the next two weeks. No time out. No socializing. Just ride, ride, ride!"

"Giddyup, here comes Billie Mason!" At lunchtime a group of boys in the cafeteria made the usual horse noises as Billie passed by.

Today she didn't care. She held her head high and headed for some girls from her class.

"Neigh!" Karl cried shrilly, slapping his thigh.

"Ignore him," Lucy muttered as Billie sat down beside her.

"Yeah, blank him," Kirsty agreed.

"Really?" Billie said, surprised.

Kirsty sniffed. "Yeah, Karl's an idiot."

"He is?" Billie clearly remembered Kirsty cozying up to Karl at Starbucks.

Lucy leaned across to whisper, "They were an item for a week, and then he dumped her."

"Ah!" Suddenly it all made sense. "Anyway, I agree—he's an idiot."

"Dissing you just because you ride horses," Kirsty grumbled as she munched a candy bar. "How stupid is that?"

"Yeah, we could just as easily diss him for playing rugby," Lucy said, making ape noises and swinging her arms like a gorilla.

Playboy Karl wasn't making many friends among the girls, Billie decided. She couldn't help feeling pleased.

"So anyway, how's the riding going?" Kirsty asked.

"Good," Billie replied. This was a surprise, too—fashionista Kirsty didn't usually take an interest in Billie's out-of-school activities.

Everyone looked at her, waiting for more.

"I'm competing at Ireton Castle on Saturday," she said, blushing. "My new trainer got me back on the selection list for the British junior team. If we do okay there, we go to Chepstow for the British junior trials."

"Wow!" Kirsty said. She and the others were genuinely impressed. "Hey, cool, Billie, you're a star!"

Saturday arrived, and it felt too soon for Billie.

"We've only been in training for less than a week," she reminded Bryony, who was coming to Ireton for moral support. Jules was resting Missie, so Billie and Val were the only combination from Matthew's stable. "I've just gotten used to the idea that we're eventing again."

"No worries!" Bryony insisted. "You kept Val in shape all winter, so that's not going to be a problem. If you keep your head on straight, you'll sail through."

"Yeah—'if'!" Billie muttered. It was a big deal to be going out there in front of the judges, pushing Val to the limit again. "I only hope I don't mess up!"

"You won't!" Bryony assured her as Sarah drove the dark red and gold Pinkerton trailer into the parking field beside the ruined castle. Behind it, green hills rose gently to a wooded area, with another range of rolling hills beyond.

It was time to spring into action—to unload Valentine's Kiss, to go and collect her number and pay the starting fee, to have her caps checked and tagged, and then to go back to Val to groom him and listen to last-minute instructions from Sarah.

"Take time before the dressage to steady Val and keep him calm. Don't let the other horses wind him up."

Billie nodded.

"And when you're doing the routine,

keep your mind on the details. Dressage is a test of concentration as much as anything, remember."

"Got it." Billie's throat felt dry. She was nervous, but not in a panic, in spite of the crowd gathered at the historic site. As usual, Val was enjoying the sense of occasion.

"He looks great," Bryony assured Billie.

"Thanks to you," Billie said. "You braided his mane better than I ever could!"

Then her name was announced over the loudspeaker system. "Number fifteen, Billie Mason on Valentine's Kiss."

Billie cantered Val into the ring, spotting her mother and father at the front of the crowd, next to the judge's box.

She looked her best in her black jacket and spotless white jodhpurs, with her long black boots and classy brimmed cap. "This feels right!" she said to herself, coming to a complete halt and saluting the judges. "Come on, Val, let's show them what we can do!"

★ ★ ★

On show, moving up from walk to trot, down the center line, and then circling to the right. Perfect so far. Billie concentrated on keeping the rhythm, working with Val on the half pass, building up to an instantaneous halt. *Take the five steps back. Good boy, Val. Now for the extended walk, the canter on a half circle, another half pass, track right into a snaking path of two loops, canter, and countercanter. Still good. We maybe dropped a point or two on the flying change—not quite straight. Never mind. Track left, extend the canter again, follow it up with another serpentine, another flying change—perfect this time.* They returned to the center line, finally coming to a halt like a statue. Billie looked at the judges and saluted. *Finish!*

The crowd applauded. Billie rode Val out of the ring.

Sarah greeted her in the waiting area and took Val's reins. She didn't say anything.

"Sorry—that bad flying change was down to me," Billie admitted.

"Yeah, you picked up a couple of penalty points, but no worries."

"I'm mad at myself, though." Billie slid off the saddle.

"Don't be. Tell Val how well he did. Be nice to him."

"Good boy," she murmured as he nuzzled her hand.

In any case, Billie had no time to worry about the dressage, because it was time to get Val ready for his show-jumping round.

Out came the fancy tail braids, and on went the tendon boots and close-contact saddle and Billie's round helmet. Before she knew it, they were being called to the show-jumping ring.

"Okay?" Sarah checked with her as she rode away.

Billie looked over her shoulder and nodded. "This isn't the part I have a problem with," she reminded her.

Sure, those fences were high, but once you were out of the novice class and into intermediate, this came with the territory. And there was tension in the crowd, whose faces you could see as you trotted around the ring, waiting for the starting bell. But everything was neatly laid out and contained—not like the wild cross-country that came next.

The bell rang and the clock started.

Okay, Val, we love these jumps. We're going to go clear, no refusals, no running out. First the nice, easy vertical—up and over. Keep a tight line toward the square spread and on to the tricky triple bar. It's wider than it looks. Steady and up at full stretch—nice, smooth landing—good boy!

Billie's mother and father were tense as they watched Billie jump. The jumps were high; the course was tight and challenging. Billie's mother kept her fingers firmly crossed.

"She's doing really well," Bryony muttered, sitting beside them at the front of the crowd. Sarah stood by the entrance to the ring, watching every move.

They cantered toward the wall. Val tucked his feet up under him at a signal from Billie, using those powerhouse muscles. *Good boy! Double combination. Watch it, Val, too fast—you clipped the first pole. Two strides and into the second. Clear again! Turn tight, keep the line over the water.* They were flying. Another sharp turn, and they took the hogs' back at a flat gallop, Billie focused on beating the clock, keeping going!

"Still clear!" Bryony murmured, holding her breath.

They were at the last fence—the triple. *Easy, boy. Up and over and land, take two strides, up again, safe landing for the final jump. Up, Val—you can do it!*

"A clear round for Billie Mason on Valentine's Kiss!" the voice on the loudspeaker announced.

Billie slowed Val to a trot. She was elated. "So good!" she told her brave horse. "What an athlete!"

"Stunning!" This time Sarah praised them both as they rode from the ring. "Honestly, Billie, you were unbelievable!"

Chapter 7

There was a long gap for lunch between show jumping and cross-country. Horses rested. Riders relaxed.

"Billie, I checked the scoreboard. You're way ahead!" Bryony reported as she brought soft drinks and sandwiches from the refreshment tent. "And I overheard two judges talking about you. They were way impressed!"

Billie sat in the cab of the trailer with Sarah. She smiled and nodded, but the elation that she'd felt after the show-jumping round had rapidly faded. Her stomach churned, and she could only nibble on her sandwich.

Sarah noticed the change of mood. She

waited a while, feet up on the dashboard, leaning back in her seat.

Billie fiddled with her food and then packed it away. She bit her lip, closed her eyes, and sighed.

"Okay, come and inspect the cross-country course with me," Sarah invited. "And while we're walking, you can tell me what's on your mind."

They walked together up the hill, past the rough log fences built into the hillside, and then through the woods, past a half coffin and a tricky upright.

"I can't help thinking about what happened to Free Spirit," Billie confessed. "I try to blank it out of my mind, but I get flashbacks. It hits me in the stomach every time!"

"I lost a horse once," Sarah confided quietly. "It was out in New Zealand. Nothing to do with wrecking his legs over a jump. Sea Spray got a bad case of colic and died."

"I'm sorry," Billie murmured. They stood at the top of the hill, gazing down at the sweeping sequence of jumps on the far side.

"If I'd gotten to him earlier, he might have made it. But he was already cast down in a corner of his stall. He'd been like that all night, which put a tremendous strain on his cardiovascular system—eventually his heart gave out."

Billie shivered. "Val means everything to me."

"I know. Losing Sea Spray was the reason I left home and came here." Sarah talked easily and openly. "I needed a fresh start."

"Lucky for me you did," Billie told her. The trainer turned and looked straight at her. "You know, to reach the top in this sport, you need to be tough. Think about it—you throw yourself over fences, through water, over ditches. You trust your horse enough to know that he'll take care of you. And he trusts that you won't ask him to do anything beyond his limits."

"Trust," Billie echoed.

"Yeah, even more than mental toughness—trust is what it's all about."

"Good luck!" Billie's dad stood close by as Billie mounted Val for the cross-country. She was dressed in a striped pale blue and white polo shirt, well shielded by her dark blue padded body protector and helmet.

"And take care," her mother added.

"Have a good one!" Bryony called as Val and Billie headed for the start.

Billie's heart beat fast. There was tension in her hands that transmitted to Val via the bridle and bit. His neck stiffened and he flicked his ears nervously. They were off.

Trust.

★ ★ ★

Ahead was the easy flower bed to give them a chance to settle in. Billie gave Val his head and let him jump freely. She felt him surge on past the flowers over a low brush fence, up toward the first big one— a mockup of the old castle in miniature, built in fake stone, with a quick right turn toward a staircase of log piles, and on again toward the woods.

Trust.

Val soared over the castle, turned toward the log piles, and galloped on. Billie's heart rate leveled off; her hands grew soft on the reins. She was beginning to settle in the saddle, feeling in control once again.

Concentrate. Jump the big ditch onto the bank, over the half-hidden log. Racing into the woods, stretch over a six-foot spread and now the angled rail over a dry ditch. Just made it. Steady, Val! The ground was softer under the trees as Billie took a little more time over the hay cart and then rattled out from under the trees down toward the pond. *Come on, Val, you like this! Go straight for the willow fence—up and splash down into the pond, hold tight, hang onto the reins.* The spray was everywhere, a cold shock. Three strides through the water, and they were out. *Amazing! Gallop across the open field to the barrels. Don't get tired now. Keep going over the gate and then swing to the right to take the coffin jump.*

"Stay focused, Billie. Trust your horse!" Sarah muttered as she stood at the finish. "Know that Valentine's Kiss is a gutsy horse. He'll run for you until his heart bursts!"

The final water lay ahead—a willow fence and a six-foot stretch over the sparkling surface. Familiar faces at the finish point were willing Billie on. *Focus. Trust. Rise up out of the saddle, soar through the air, land without even a splash.*

We did it!

As Valentine's Kiss cruised toward the finish, the last shred of doubt cleared from Billie's mind.

Chapter 8

"We have high hopes," Matthew Pinkerton told Billie's dad.

It was the Wednesday following Ireton, and news had come through that the selectors had invited Billie and Val to Chepstow.

"She did pretty well," Mr. Mason acknowledged. "We were on the edge of our seats all day, hoping that she'd put in enough preparation to get through. Luckily, she did it."

"Thanks to Sarah," Billie added. As usual, she wished her dad wouldn't talk about her as if she wasn't there.

"Jules will be at Chepstow with Mission Impossible, so we'll have two competitors from the stable," Matthew told them.

Mr. Mason nodded. "That'll keep you on your toes, Billie."

"Actually, we get along really well—remember?" Billie muttered. "But guess who else is going to be there? Some of the kids from school say they're coming to cheer me on."

The conversation at school had gone like this:

Tuesday. Lunch break.

Kirsty: Hey, Billie, what are you looking so pleased about?

Billie: I've got a place at the British junior trials. The letter came this morning.

Kirsty: Cool! Did you hear that, Lucy? Billie's going to be on the British eventing team.

Karl *(listening in from across the room):* Neigh! Giddyup!

Kirsty: Shut up, Karl!

Lucy: That's amazing, Billie.

Billie: I'm not in yet. It all depends on

how I perform at Chepstow.

Kirsty: Can we come and watch?

Billie *(surprised):* It's a long way. Are you sure?

Kirsty: It's a school holiday. My brother Tom will drive us. It'll be a great day out.

Lucy: We'll cheer for you, Billie. We'll hold up banners with your name on them.

Billie came back to the present to find Matthew talking to her.

"In that case, you have no time to lose." He looked over to where Sarah was leading Valentine's Kiss out of his stall. "It looks like you have some work to do!"

"Last Saturday you lost impulsion on the first serpentine in the dressage test," Sarah told Billie. "You dropped a couple of marks there, so we're going to iron that one out now."

Billie nodded. "I didn't make the curve, did I?"

"No. Make sure you take the loop right

out to the side of the ring. That's good. This is a collected canter, with plenty of forward movement. Better—Billie, your position is perfect; hold that—yes, nice work!"

At the end of the exercise, Billie trotted to join her trainer. "After we've finished in here, can I go through a couple of points with you in the show-jumping ring?"

Sarah shook her head. "I know you're eager, but don't try to do too much, okay? The best thing would be for you to ride Val out for an hour to give him some exercise."

Billie was disappointed, but she knew Sarah was right. *I can't expect my trainer to give me all her time*, she thought.

In any case, Chepstow was still a week and a half away, and the trail ride turned out to be fun. She, Bryony, and Jules chilled out and had a laugh.

On Sunday, Sarah showed Billie and Val

how to perfect the shoulder-in left and left tracking for the dressage test. They practiced over and over again until they got the angle just right, until the steps were perfectly smooth and regular.

On Monday evening, they were in the show-jumping ring, tightening up the technicalities of the turns, varying the distances between fences so that Billie could work on adjusting Val's long stride.

They rested the horses on Tuesday, and then on Wednesday, Sarah drove Billie and Jules, Val, and Missie out to Orton Park to use a neighbor's cross-country course. They pushed their horses over big hanging oxers, turning first left and then right, over lumpy ground down to curved steps cut into the bank, testing their horses' scope and accuracy.

Sarah was pleased with their performances. "Your horses are working really well for you," she told the girls. "On the weekend I want you both to go out there and have fun!"

Then there was the final dressage workout on Thursday, the plan being to rest the horses again on Friday. But when Billie got to the stable, Sarah was nowhere to be found.

"Sarah's not here," Matthew said abruptly when Billie asked him about her. "You and Jules will be working with me today."

"Is she okay?" Billie asked, but Matthew was already walking away.

Billie sighed as she went off to the tack room for Val's saddle. Matthew was a top trainer, but he didn't have Sarah's laid-back style. The young trainer was inspirational, and Billie would miss her.

"I know—Sarah should be working with us," she murmured to Val as she slung the saddle over his back and tightened the girth. "I'm wondering what's up, just like you! But there are a hundred things we still need to work on before Chepstow!"

Joey Hicks came in then with Val's gleaming bridle and offered unasked-for advice on the type of bit that Billie should be using.

"Where's Sarah?" Billie asked as she tacked up Val.

Joey grunted. "She was on a trail ride on Hawksmoor earlier today. A tractor roared around a bend in the lane and scared the horse badly. Sarah took a fall. They carted her off to the hospital."

"It's nothing serious, is it?" Billie asked.

Joey shrugged and offered to lead Val out to the dressage ring where Matthew and Jules were already working with Missie. Billie followed him, troubled.

I hope she's okay, Billie thought. *Anyway, Matthew always sends you off to the hospital to get checked out after a fall. It'll probably turn out to be nothing.*

"Come on, Billie!" Matthew called. "We're going through our entrance here. Collected canter into halt and then the salute."

Billie found that working with Matthew again was strange after her sessions with Sarah. Matthew's style was brisker and more businesslike. He seemed to favor Jules and Mission Impossible and then find small faults in Val and Billie's performance.

"Keep that hind leg engaged on the half circle left," he yelled after their first flying change. "That was messy, Billie. I want you to try it again—from the beginning!"

She nodded and went back to the start, even though she could sense that Val was tiring. This time they got the flying change right but lost impulsion later in the routine. The session ended with lukewarm praise from Matthew.

"Jules, concentrate on Missie's attention and obedience. She sometimes ignores your contact with the bit. Billie, it's the opposite with Val—you occasionally don't get him moving forward smoothly enough. Lots to work on, both of you!"

"Phew!" As Jules rode out of the ring, she

shook her head. "We were terrible. Shall we just give in and admit defeat now?"

"No way!" Billie argued with a laugh. "We both have to show Matthew that we can do it. Besides, Sarah wouldn't have been that hard on us if she'd been here."

"Hey, Joey!" Jules called the stable boy as she dismounted ouside the barn. "Why isn't Sarah back yet?"

"She's a bit ill," Joey grunted. For once he seemed unwilling to talk.

"What's wrong with her?" Jules persisted.

"I can't say."

Jules led Missie into her stall while Billie dismounted from Val.

"Can't say or won't say?" Jules quizzed.

"They don't know yet," Joey told her. "They're doing tests."

Billie tucked Val's stirrups out of the way and led him into his stall. She came quickly out again. "Who's doing tests?" she wanted to know. "What kind of tests?"

"The hospital." Under the two-pronged

pressure, Joey delivered the information through gritted teeth. "Tests on her spine. They say that they'll have to keep her in."

Jules glanced at Billie. "Sounds like it could be serious," she muttered.

"Did she really hurt herself when she fell?" Billie asked, white-faced.

"Landed badly," Joey said. "She was a bit woozy when the ambulance came. It's probably nothing."

Billie closed her eyes and bit her lip. *It can't be serious!* she told herself. *They'll let her out of the hospital, and she'll be at Chepstow with us, just like we planned!*

But she felt uneasy when she went home, trying to picture her healthy, outdoorsy trainer cooped up in a hospital, waiting for the results.

"It's our last day at school today before the break," Billie reminded her mother when she got up the following morning. "Can you write me a note to let me leave early so that I can go to visit Sarah at the hospital?"

Her mother hesitated. "I don't like you missing school, Billie."

"We're breaking up today, so we won't be doing any work," Billie insisted. "I'm worried about Sarah!"

Eventually her mother agreed, and early in the afternoon Billie was walking down a long, shiny hospital corridor, following the signs to Unit G.

"Third door on the left," the nurse told her when she asked for Sarah Norwood.

Sarah was lying flat, looking up at the ceiling. Her neck was supported by a brace so that she couldn't turn it. Billie edged over toward the bed.

"Hi," she said quietly.

"Hey, Billie!" Sarah said, looking pleased to see her. "I take it you and Val are ready for the big event!"

"As ready as we'll ever be." Billie sat down awkwardly by the bed. "But when are they going to let you out of here? Are you going to be able to come with us?"

"Somehow I doubt it, because of that stupid fall. The tractor spooked Hawksmoor bigtime. I went flying." She looked up at the ceiling and sighed. "I don't know when they're going to let me get out of bed, let alone leave the hospital."

There was a silence while Billie gradually took this in. "Is it really bad?"

"I've got a tingling sensation in my hands and my feet are numb," Sarah said candidly. "They've been doing tests, but there's too much swelling for them to be able to tell if there's anything seriously wrong with my spine. It might just be bruised. I have to wait and see if things improve over the next couple of days."

Billie looked around the room at Sarah's fellow patients, at the nurses coming and going with trolleys, at the trees growing outside the window in the hospital grounds. It seemed all wrong that her tanned, outdoors-loving trainer should be flat on her back in the hospital. "What happens if there is something wrong with your spine?" she asked.

Sarah made a face. "I might not be able to do the things I used to do. They think I'll be okay to walk—but I might never be able to ride again!"

Billie's heart thumped against her ribs. "I don't know what to say!"

"There's no need to say anything. I'm still getting used to it myself."

"Can I do anything?"

"No thanks, Billie. It's good of you to visit. To tell you the truth, you're the one person I really wanted to see."

"I am?"

"Yes. I wanted to say good luck at Chepstow."

Billie frowned. "But I can't go—not now!" *Not without you!*

"Sure you can," Sarah insisted. "I guessed you might react this way, but honestly, you don't need me to be there. I already taught you and Val everything I know."

"I can't—I don't want to—it wouldn't be the same!" There were tears in Billie's eyes. She clasped her hands on her lap and let her head fall forward.

"Billie, don't." For the first time Sarah's voice broke down. But then she took a deep breath and got control of her voice again. "Don't cry. I'm going to get better—okay?"

Billie nodded slowly.

"I've just got to rest and wait until the swelling goes down. I've got a feeling that everything is going to be fine." She waited for Billie to look up. "Before you know it, I'll be back at that stable dishing out the orders, getting you and Valentine's Kiss ready for Europe!"

"Promise?"

"I promise. But only if you get yourself along to Chepstow tomorrow. That's the deal."

Billie bit her lip and then nodded. "Okay."

Sarah looked her in the eye. "Listen to me. You'll take Val and you'll go out there and show the judges exactly what you can do."

"Deal!" she murmured.

"And you'll do it for me," she urged. "I'll be here and I'll be urging you on in my imagination on every flying change, over every triple combination, through every water splash. I'll be with you every inch of the way!"

Chapter 9

"Jules, help Joey lower the ramp. Billie and Bryony, stand well back!" Matthew gave out the orders as the team arrived at Chepstow. "Good. Now, Billie, let Jules get in there and lead Missie out first. Easy does it."

Missie came noisily and nervously out of the trailer. She pranced and danced down the ramp onto the soft ground.

"Okay, Billie, your turn!"

Billie went in and untied Val's rope. "Easy, boy," she murmured, softly stroking his nose. "You're so good! Nice and easy does it, come on, down the ramp."

Val walked carefully out of the trailer and then looked up and around the vast parking field. At 7:30 in the morning, it was already full of trailers. Eventers of every color, all in beautiful condition, were safely tethered after their journeys and munching hay.

"Stand!" Jules ordered her restless chestnut mare. Missie had sweated a lot in the trailer and hadn't traveled well. Matthew told Joey to sponge her down and settle her.

"Billie, I'll help you with Val," Bryony offered. "He's looking good. The hustle and bustle doesn't seem to bother him."

"He likes it," Billie said. "This is a big day for us. He knows that he has to be on his best behavior."

"You hear that, Val?" Bryony opened the grooming box and took out a comb. "I'm going to braid you and make you look extra handsome today!"

As Bryony worked on Val, Billie went off with Jules to join the line for their numbers. Ahead of them were Angie

Booth and Dom Carthy from Roger Goodman's stable in Northern Ireland.

"Hey, you two!" Dom spotted them and turned to chat. "Long time no see, Billie!"

"I was at Ireton," she answered. Dom was into mind games, always trying to find a way to put other riders down.

"We didn't bother with that one," he said, dismissing it with a quiet click of his tongue. "We reckoned we'd already done enough for the selectors at earlier events. It turns out that we were right."

As Dom took his bib and went to have his caps checked, a girl standing behind Billie and Jules sighed. "Is it just me or is Dominic Carthy totally into himself?"

"It isn't and he is!" Jules said, grinning.

"But he's a good rider, too," Billie reminded them. "I reckon he and Allegro have the dressage section sewn up before they even set foot in the ring."

"Don't say that!" Jules protested. "I didn't get out of bed at four o'clock this morning to hear that we don't have the faintest chance of grabbing the selectors' attention!"

"That's not what I said. But, let's face it, it's only six out of sixty-five combinations that get chosen," Billie insisted. "We've got less than a one-in-ten chance."

"I'm out of here!" Jules sighed, taking her number and striding off. "If I hang around with you much longer, Billie, I'll lose the will to live!"

"I was only being realistic." Billie told Bryony what Jules had said.

They were putting the finishing touches on Val's braids and brushing him until his dappled coat was as smooth as silk.

"Yeah, but you do seem a bit down, considering this is the biggest weekend of your life," Bryony pointed out. "You know—kind of quiet."

"I keep thinking about Sarah," Billie

confessed. "I can't believe this is happening to her. She doesn't deserve it."

Bryony nodded. "I know. She's a cool person."

"And she's a brilliant trainer. She knows horses better than anyone I've ever met!"

"Sshh—don't let Matthew hear you say that!"

"It's true. Matthew's good. But he doesn't understand Val the way Sarah does. Sarah looks at every little movement; she reads Val's body language. Honestly, Bryony, I miss her being here, and so does Val!"

"So get out there and win for Sarah," Bryony told her. "It's the best news you could possibly give her!"

Billie nodded. She stood back from Val to admire the finished effect. "That's what Sarah said when I saw her at the hospital yesterday," she murmured. "So I guess that's what we're going to go out there and do!"

★ ★ ★

"Contact, contact, contact!" Matthew gave Jules her final instruction before she rode into the dressage ring. She was the last to go before lunch, and it had been a long wait for the edgy horse and rider.

Billie sat ringside and watched Missie canter into view. She saw Jules halt and salute the judges.

"That's a new horse for Jules, isn't it?" Dom leaned forward from the row behind.

Billie nodded. So far the test was going well for Jules. Missie's transitions were smooth; her rein back was perfect.

"What happened to her last horse?" Dom asked, faking forgetfulness. "Oh, I remember—she fell on the cross-country, didn't she? I wasn't there, but you were, Billie. Did the horse have to be destroyed?"

"Sshh!" Bryony warned.

Billie frowned. Dom Carthy knew exactly what had happened to Free Spirit. This was just one of his mind games—

reminding her of bad things in order put her off her game. By coincidence as he spoke, Jules picked up a couple of penalty points on a flying change into collected canter.

Dom saw it, too. "Pity about that," he said, leaning back and smiling smugly.

"Impulsion!" Matthew reminded Billie after lunch.

Billie had tacked Val up with Joey's help. As she predicted, she was chasing a near-perfect score by Dom and Allegro. Out there in the crowd were her mother and father, but there was no sign so far of Kirsty and the gang from school. So much for their promises to cheer her on!

"Keep him moving forward, keep him supple, and above all, keep his hindquarters engaged!"

Billie nodded slowly. She slid her left foot into the stirrup and mounted smoothly. *Do it for me!* she heard Sarah tell her.

The bell rang, and she cantered into the ring.

I'll be with you every step of the way!

Billie rode with the softest of touches, hoping to make it look easy. *Read Val's strides, think three steps ahead.*

She sat straight in the saddle, head up, looking forward, adjusted the reins, and put gentle pressure on, first with the right leg and then the left. She kept her movements relaxed and easy.

Good boy, Val! Move forward into the half pass right and half pass left. Perfect! Into walk, still looking straight ahead, gentle hands on the reins. Billie was reading Val's body language. *Perfect again on the rein back, now forward and lengthen out into extended walk, showing off an elegant line.* Billie urged Val on again, in canter from that point until the finish—they collected, extended, and then collected again, following up with serpentines and flying changes. *Halt. Good boy! Stand and salute!*

★ ★ ★

Hey, Sarah, Billie texted from her bunkhouse that evening. *Dressage went well. Lost 2 marks on 1st serpentine, 3 on half pass left, and 5 in collective. In 3rd place behind Dom Carthy and Paula Howard. Jules in 5th. Hope you're OK—luv, Billie*

"Did you hear from Sarah?" Bryony asked Billie early the next morning. They were up and showered before most of the other girls, including Jules.

"No. I texted her, but I didn't get a reply."

"Oh. Come to think of it, she probably can't use her phone in the hospital."

"Yeah." Billie clasped her hair back from her face and pulled a long-sleeved polo shirt over her head and then went out to feed Val and Missie. After that she walked the show-jumping course with Matthew to plan her ride.

"Keep Val steady and take time to find

the best line, especially between the triple bar and the wall," he advised. "Billie, did you hear what I said?"

She nodded quickly.

"No need to go like mad unless there's a jump-off," he added.

Trust your horse, Sarah's voice said. "I'll let him go at his own pace," she promised Matthew. "I won't force him to do anything he doesn't want to do."

Day two brought the crowds to the show-jumping ring. The sun shone, but there was a stiff breeze—good conditions to cool the pressure-cooker atmosphere that was building up as the selectors took their seats.

"It's a tough course," Billie's mother said. She and Billie's dad were sitting three rows back.

"That's good. It'll sort out the wheat from the chaff," he pointed out confidently.

Farther along the row, a group of girls unfurled a banner. It read, "Go, Billie, go!"

"Look, Billie has a fan club!" Mrs. Mason was thrilled.

"Has Billie been on yet?" Lucy nudged Kirsty and fidgeted in her seat. They'd set off late, thanks to Kirsty's brother Tom. "Did we miss her?"

"No, stupid. She's not on for ages yet. Look at the program—her name comes near the end."

"Here's a black horse now," Lucy cried as a competitor rode into the ring. "What color is Billie's? What's its name again?"

"Valentine's Kiss," Kirsty read from the program. "I told you—this isn't her. Anyway, hush, Lucy—you'll scare the poor horse!"

"And that's a clear round for Paula Howard on Maximilian III!" the announcer boomed over the noise of the crowd. ". . . A four-point penalty for a refusal and six time penalties for Kit Roberts on Blue Chip puts him into ninth place . . . Another clear, this time for Angie Booth on Charlie Boy . . . And number thirty-six, Paul Braddock on Salad Days, has withdrawn from the competition, making way for Jules Carter on Mission Impossible."

"You're pulling too hard on the reins," Matthew muttered as Jules rode forward. Missie pranced and fought for her head. "You're hurting her mouth!"

"Easy, Jules!" Billie whispered.

Jules seemed to heed the advice. She relaxed the reins and let Missie walk around the ring until the bell rang. They were off! But then she got another attack of nerves. Instead of riding Missie steadily at the first easy vertical, she rushed it and clipped the bar.

"Ooh!" A small gasp came from the crowd, but the pole stayed in place.

Rushing again, Jules cleared a hogs'

back and a combination and then turned sharply for the open water jump.

"Too tight!" Matthew warned.

Missie was off balance and wary of the gleaming water. She stopped short and refused to jump. Jules turned her and tried again. This time they were safely over. But again they were off balance coming up to the largest oxer on the course. Jules drove Missie on. The horse tried to put in an extra stride, but instead of soaring over the jump, crashed into it.

Horse and rider were down, rolling on the ground, struggling to get up. There was a short silence and then a sudden buzz of noise in the crowd as Jules caught hold of Missie's reins and remounted.

"Missie's okay—she's fine!" Matthew muttered anxiously. He signaled for Jules to complete the course.

Jules and Missie went on and made it over the last three fences. They rode out to sympathetic applause, but Jules's face was ashen and her breathing uneven as she dismounted. She handed the reins to Matthew and walked off without a word.

Quickly, Billie followed and caught up with Jules outside their trailer. "Are you okay? Did you hurt yourself?"

"Only my pride," Jules whispered. She sat on the ramp, her head in her hands.

"You got straight back up," Billie insisted. "No way did you make a fool of yourself."

But Jules shook her head. "I messed up. And everyone saw. I might as well pack up and go home right now!"

"Listen, Jules, I'll talk to you later, okay?" Checking her watch, Billie saw that it was time for her to compete. At this rate she'd miss her turn and be disqualified. "I have to go. Wish me luck!"

She dashed back across the field, through the tents and lines for the portable toilets, to the ring where Joey waited for her with Val.

"A clear round for Dominic Carthy on Allegro!" came the announcement as Billie mounted. "And now, in third place at the end of the dressage section, Billie Mason on her six-year-old gelding, Valentine's Kiss!"

Chapter 10

Okay, Val, this is huge! Mess this up and we're nowhere!

Billie gathered herself and walked her horse easily into the show-jumping ring. They passed Dom Carthy on his way out.

"We went clear, no problem!" he boasted. "Allegro's been in top form all season. No one's even gotten close to her scores so far."

"She's a good little horse," Billie acknowledged. At 15.5 hands, Allegro needed a big heart and lots of courage to compete with leggy jumpers like Val. *Nice mare—pity about the rider!* she thought darkly as she and Val waited for the bell.

Sitting there, waiting for the signal, Billie

told herself to concentrate. She couldn't let Jules's fall or Dominic's cockiness get to her. *Think of Sarah!*

Up and over the first vertical, forward in the saddle for the takeoff, lean back as we land. Nice and smooth. Now the hogs' back and an easy combination, getting into our stride. Well done, Val—no problem, as Dom would say. On again, Val making six strides before flying over the first oxer and then making a tight, controlled turn toward the triple. They were jumping big—flying again! Val tucked his front legs under him for the next combination, keeping to his own rhythm, enjoying the moment.

They were still clear and had lots of time in hand. The wall was big; Billie gave herself time to judge it properly, making seconds back on the turn into the last oxer. *Over. Race for the line!*

Billie and Val went clear.

"Go, Billie, go!" Kirsty and the gang

chanted loudly.

It was a four-way jump-off between Billie, Paula, Angie, and Dom. The fences were raised. It was a race against the clock.

"This isn't Billie—it's Paula Thingy on Max-i-thingy." It was Lucy's turn to put the girls right, even if she wasn't altogether clear on the details!

Paula came into the ring and rode her black gelding hard. She cleared the vertical and the double and was going well. But she cut corners and charged Maximilian straight into the water, losing time when she had to turn him around and take it again.

"We can beat that!" Billie told Val as they waited in the warm-up ring.

Angie was chosen to go next, then Billie, then Dom. Billie saw that Charlie Boy was on edge, charging forward into the ring and napping badly as the bell rang and Angie went hard at the vertical. It was a disaster from the start—the first pole was down, then the second. Angie and Charlie were losing points down the central run, completely out of it by the time they hit the water.

"Well, what do you know—it's between you and me, Billie!" Dom commented calmly as they watched the fences being rebuilt. "You watch yourself over that big wall, you hear?"

Billie rode out and waited for the bell. She could feel the tension in the air.

"Go, Billie!" Kirsty's voice rose above the general hum.

"You hear that?" Billie whispered in Val's ear. She smiled to herself but didn't let the distraction get to her. *Thanks, Kirsty—you made it!*

Val pricked his ears toward the first fence. At the sound of the bell he launched himself forward.

Clear and clear and clear! It was like a dream. Val raced on, tucked neatly around the bends, flew over the poles. *Gallop and jump, turn again, take the wall—completely flying, never putting a foot wrong. Oxers and rail-ditch-rail combinations, the water, the wall, the last tricky run of fences. Clear!*

The crowd cheered them out of the ring. Billie didn't look at Dom as he rode past her, the last competitor in the jump-off.

Trust your horse—Sarah's words of wisdom rang inside her head. She was right, as always.

Clear in the jump-off, Billie texted her as soon as she dismounted.

Dom Carthy rode clear, too, but in a longer time. He held on to first place in the overall competition, while Billie moved up to second.

It was Sunday evening, and everything now depended on the third day and the cross-country challenge.

"I won't ride tomorrow," Jules said firmly when Billie caught up with her in the bunkhouse.

"What are you saying? Does Matthew know about this?" Billie asked.

"No, I haven't told him yet."

It was dusk. The crowd had long since dispersed. Only the competing teams stayed to tend their horses and get a good night's sleep before the final day.

Billie was shocked. "Do you mean you're pulling out completely?"

Jules nodded. "The selectors aren't going to choose me—not after I messed up today."

"You don't know that for sure," Billie argued, sitting on the bunk next to Jules. "You could ride the cross-country and get back into the top six—there's definitely still a chance for you and Missie!"

"No way," Jules said with a sigh.

"Yes, there is!" Billie was determined not to let Jules cave in so easily.

"Listen, something happened to me out there today." Jules's confession was so quiet that Billie had to strain to hear. "All the bad stuff from last year came flooding back.

Maybe it was the sound of the poles crashing down or the sight of Missie rolling over and looking as if she'd never get back up."

"But she did—you both did! You got back on and finished the course."

Jules shrugged and then managed a faint smile. "Do you realize how weird this is?"

"What?"

"I lose my nerve and you do your best to help me out—after the way I treated you a few weeks ago!"

Billie shook her head. "It did me good," she insisted. "It made me face my demons, as Sarah would say." Billie let a silence develop and then went on. "You know, your demons are the same as mine—it's the nightmare that you might make a mistake and hurt your horse. You'd never forgive yourself if it happened again."

"It's true—I wouldn't." Jules felt the old despair grab hold of her.

"Then listen to what Sarah told me,"

Billie urged. "She said, 'Trust your horse.' I mean, did you ever hear of a horse in the wild that tried to jump something it knew it couldn't handle?"

"No," Jules agreed quietly. "But it's too soon for Missie and me to make the sort of team you and Val make. It takes years."

"Just trust her," Billie said again. "You're a great rider, Jules. And she's a powerful, gutsy horse. Go with the flow and know that Missie will keep herself safe."

Jules closed her eyes and thought through Billie's advice. "I want to believe you," she said slowly.

"It's not me you have to believe—it's Sarah."

"Yes—Sarah!" There was a sad silence while they thought of the absent trainer. Then, "Okay, I'll do it," Jules decided. "Don't mention a word to Matthew about what I've just said."

"I promise," Billie told her. "We'll get through our cross-country problems together, Jules, you wait and see!"

Day three, and everyone's nerves were stretched to the breaking point.

As the riders prepared their horses for the cross-country, the crowds wandered across the fields, deciding where to stand for the best view.

"I didn't wear the right shoes!" Lucy complained, her ballet slippers sinking into the soft turf beside the lake. They'd made the effort to come again, hoping to see their friend snatch the top spot.

"Stop complaining," Kirsty muttered as she unfurled her "Go, Billie, go!" banner and waited for the action to begin.

Meanwhile, Billie's parents were having a chat with their daughter.

"Whatever happens today, we're proud of you," her mother said. "The way you've made your comeback says a lot about you!"

Billie busily checked Val's neat white saddle pad and matching kick boots.

"Thanks, Mum," she said quietly.

"It takes great strength of character to turn things around the way you have," her dad agreed.

Billie smiled awkwardly. "Dad, could you make it sound less like I was a private in the army and you were my colonel in chief?" But hey, why change the habit of a lifetime? Her smile broadened into a grin.

"Well, good luck," her mother and father chorused as she mounted.

"Good luck!" Joey told her.

"Good luck, Billie!" Bryony stood by the Pinkerton trailer.

Matthew took hold of the reins and led Val and Billie into the practice ring, where Jules was already waiting tensely for her turn.

"We're next to go," she whispered, keeping a wary lookout for the official signal.

"Remember the Sarah message!" Billie muttered.

The girls did a high-five. "Trust your horse!" they chorused.

"Did you hear from her?" Jules asked hastily. The official was beckoning her toward the start. She glanced back for Billie's answer.

"No." Sarah's silence was the one shadow over this nervy, exciting, hold-your-breath, cross-your-fingers final day. Sarah—trapped in the hospital, enduring the biggest fight of all.

"Go, girl!" Billie yelled after Jules as Missie galloped up the hill.

"How did they do?" Billie asked.

She and Matthew waited as Bryony ran toward the practice ring with news of Jules's ride.

"They got around!" Bryony reported breathlessly. "Jules almost came off at the hollow, but she managed to stay in the saddle. They lost time at the lake complex because Jules took the longer, safer route."

"Sounds like she rode sensibly," Matthew said. "A wise decision."

Billie wondered if Jules and Missie had done enough. "Will it get her into the final six?"

Matthew shrugged. "If not this year, there's always next year."

At last Billie spotted a weary Jules and Missie heading toward the field where the trailers were parked. They were splattered with mud, and Missie was sweating heavily, but Jules had a broad grin on her face as they passed by.

"We did it, thanks to you!" she called to Billie. "Hey, listen! I gave Dominic a dirty look as he and Allegro set out. Let's hope it put him off!"

"Abracadabra!" Joey muttered, climbing the fence and striding after Jules to help her look after Missie.

Matthew laughed. "It'll take more than a magician's spell to keep Dominic Carthy off the British junior team!" he said to Billie.

★ ★ ★

Alone in the practice ring, Billie's stomach tightened. Dom was going well, judging by the crowd's loud shouts and cheers.

"But let's see if we can knock him from that top spot," she muttered to Val as the seconds ticked by. "I wish Sarah was here right now! Listen to that—they're cheering again. If Sarah was here, she'd be telling me to relax. No tension in the neck and back. Soft hands."

Val shifted uneasily beneath her.

Then the phone in the pocket of Billie's body protector buzzed. She flicked it open and read the message.

Hey, Billie. Sarah here. Remember—ditch those cross-country blues. Do it for me!

Here we go—the best ride of our lives!

The last-minute text message from Sarah had lit up Billie's mood and boosted her flagging confidence. She galloped Val toward the first brush hedge. The whole course lay open before them—the high log piles and wide oxers, the deep ditches and hollows, the steep banks, sunken roads, and dreaded lake.

Stay balanced, Billie told herself. *Ride the rough ground, swing right toward the first log pile. Wow, it's huge! Jump, Val, jump!* She kept his stride at the same pace and cut straight through to the open ditch, ignoring the long route. Val stretched to fly over it, clear of the rails. *Beautiful boy!* Billie thought.

She felt the wind batter them sideways as they swung right again to approach a steep bank. It put Val off his stride, so he was unprepared for the log below. He faltered and lost speed.

Billie kept him steady, worrying whether they could recover. They bounced back over the next log, focused on the task, tackling the obstacles that the course's tricky designers had placed in their way.

Now around this tree to jump the next

log—easy to miss, but we made it. Stay focused—we're not done yet!

The grassy ground blurred beneath Val's feet. The wind whipped against them. The lake gleamed in the valley below. *No runouts, no penalties so far. Zigzag over the birch poles, bounce, and turn toward a wide table jump—no problem. Take no notice of a stray plastic bag whisking across the course— don't spook—good boy!*

One hanging log, now two, and then three! A 45-degree turn toward the lake. Go for it! There was a big drop down over a bank, Billie's stomach flipping as she hung onto the reins. They ignored the crowd, keeping their pace up toward the high brush fence. They galloped downhill and launched themselves over the brush, taking the maximum drop into the lake.

There was an enormous splash, with glittering drops showering over their heads. Val took three strides across the water and bounced out over two logs. *Fantastic!*

Close to home now, but not too eager. Steady up, over the big brush corner, swing toward the finish. She could see the sea of faces, hear the cheers of the crowd. Her ears were filled with the sound of hooves thundering toward the main arena, where people waited—trainers, friends, families . . .

Home safe! Our best ride ever! The closest to heaven we could ever hope to be!

Chapter 11

"This is a photo of me and Val at the lake." Billie handed the picture to Sarah. "The photographer caught the exact moment when the spray showered down on us."

It was Sarah's first time back at the stable since she'd come out of the hospital. She looked pale and thin and limped slightly as she walked, but the smile on her face told its own story.

"Cool picture," she said.

"We had a fantastic time at Chepstow," Billie told her trainer. "Val flew around the cross-country. We shaved seconds off our time wherever we could and came in way ahead of Dom Carthy. It got us first place."

Sarah grinned at her. "Keep talking," she said.

"I didn't think about Free Spirit—not once!"

"And?"

"I was totally focused. I just lived the moment with Val."

Sarah nodded and then led her toward Val's stall.

"He's an amazing horse. Beautiful—strong—clever . . ." Billie said dreamily.

"That's you she's talking about," Sarah told Val. "And this is the girl who swore she'd never take you eventing ever again!"

Billie's face flushed red. "That was the first time we met. I was going through a bad patch."

"And now you're on top of the world—number one on the selectors' list for Europe."

"With Jules and Missie on the reserve list and Matthew going around telling everybody what a great stable he runs. My friends at school think I'm the business, and Mum and Dad are really excited that there's going to be an article about me in the local paper!"

"You hear that?" Sarah said to Val. "And all this has happened while I've been away!"

Val nudged Sarah's shoulder and then lowered his head to rummage in the trainer's pocket.

"No treats!" Sarah said sternly. "Just because you're currently the top junior eventer in the country doesn't mean we have to spoil you!"

Billie stood back and smiled. "Take a look on the other side," she told Val.

Val sniffed around until Sarah produced an apple from her pocket. "Okay, you win!"

"I'm glad you're back, Sarah," Billie said with a sigh. "Can we work together for the rest of the summer? Will you be on the British training team with us? Are you well enough to train?" The questions hung in the air.

"One day at a time," Sarah cautioned, glancing up at the wispy white clouds in the deep blue sky. "The doctors say they're pretty happy with me, though. With any luck, I should be back in the saddle in a couple of weeks."

"That's good," Billie said quietly.

"I have to have more physical therapy, but it shouldn't stop me from working with you and Val."

"Cool!"

Val snickered and gave Sarah another nudge.

"He agrees!" Billie laughed. Then she grew serious. "Isn't it weird how things change?"

Sarah nodded. "One day we clear all the fences, no problem."

"The next we bring them crashing down!"

"One minute you're on the ground . . ."

"The next, you're riding high!" Billie

finished, a smile on her face.

"Great, isn't it?" Sarah said with a grin of her own.

"Totally cool," Billie agreed.